GHOSTS

HORRIBLE HISTORIES.

TERRY DEARY

ILLUSTRATED BY
MARTIN BROWN

GHOSTS

READ ALL ABOUT THE NASTY BITS!

SCHOLASTIC

First published in the UK by Scholastic, 2022
This edition published, 2024
Scholastic, Bosworth Avenue, Warwick, CV34 6UQ
Scholastic Ireland, 89E Lagan Road, Dublin Industrial Estate, Glasnevin, Dublin, D11 HP5F

SCHOLASTIC and associated logos are trademarks and/or registered trademarks of Scholastic Inc.

Text © Terry Deary, 2022
Cover and inside illustrations © Martin Brown, 2022

The moral rights of the author and illustrator have been asserted by them.

ISBN 978 0702 32290 7

A CIP catalogue record for this book is available from the British Library.

Printed in the UK
Paper made from wood grown in sustainable forests and other controlled sources.

MIX
Paper | Supporting responsible forestry
FSC® C018072
www.fsc.org

1 3 5 7 9 10 8 6 4 2

www.scholastic.co.uk

For safety or quality concerns:
UK: www.scholastic.co.uk/productinformation
EU: www.scholastic.ie/productinformation

WHAT'S INSIDE?

FREE: Tips on how to get that ghost
see page 43–45

EXCLUSIVE: How to fake a ghost
see page 63

INTRODUCTION

As Mr Pimm will tell his class, there have been ghost STORIES since the first human storytellers told tales by the crackling fires in their dark, shadowy caves.

There are people who are scared of the dark and 'see' a ghost because they EXPECT to see a ghost.

Then there are people who will SHOW others a ghost because some people WANT to believe in ghosts. Usually, the people who let you meet a ghost are FRAUDS. They will take money from people who want to speak to a spirit.

And there are people who will tell you a ghost story because the world loves ghost stories. Some people LIKE to feel a shiver of fear. They are writers of books and films and plays.

And in history there have been thousands of ghostly mistakes, wicked frauds and super stories.

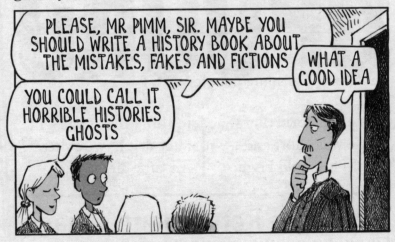

Oh dear. What a daft idea.

ANCIENT SPOOKS

In prehistoric times life was short and harsh. It would be nice to think there was a life after death, wouldn't it? An 'afterlife'?

Afterlife Retirement Village

Spooktacular care services for all you ghouls and gals in your twilight years

Visit us on our open day, this Frightday

PREHISTORIC TIMELINE

2500 BC Stone circles like Stonehenge are built. All around there are graves with treasures for the dead people. They must have believed the dead had a spirit that moved to an afterlife. Spirits means ghosts.

1323 BC Pharaoh Tutankhamun of Egypt dies. He will become part of many ghost stories.

753 BC The city of Rome begins and will grow into the Roman Empire.

700 BC Celts arrive in Britain from ancient Europe.

427–348 BC Great Greek cities grow, and teacher Plato says the body rots, but the 'soul' goes on. How does he know? Who knows?

AWFUL ASSYRIAN

Around the world people believed bodies had to rest in peace. If you disturbed a corpse, then the spirits could not rest in the afterlife – they would appear and haunt the living. Rich corpses were buried with treasures and helpful things like chariots.

The poor were buried and left to rot. The afterlife was open to the rich. The millions of poor must have been waiting outside the gates.

WE'RE POOR, COLD AND HUNGRY IN LIFE—AND IN DEATH

NOT FAIR

Ashurbanipal was king of Assyria (668–630 BC), and a cruel ruler. On his tomb he described how he treated his Egyptian enemies … in life AND after death.

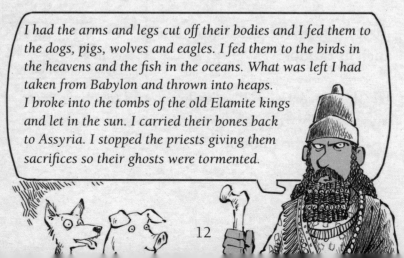

I had the arms and legs cut off their bodies and I fed them to the dogs, pigs, wolves and eagles. I fed them to the birds in the heavens and the fish in the oceans. What was left I had taken from Babylon and thrown into heaps. I broke into the tombs of the old Elamite kings and let in the sun. I carried their bones back to Assyria. I stopped the priests giving them sacrifices so their ghosts were tormented.

Poor old ghosts. But Ashurbanipal didn't seem to be bothered by ghosts.

EGYPTIAN EVILS

When ancient Egyptian mummies were dug up, the diggers were said to be haunted by the VERY old ghosts of the dead. It's said the ghosts brought disaster to them. A 'Curse of the Mummy's Tomb' sort of thing.

THE HAUNTED HAND

Egyptian king Akhenaten (1351–1334 BC) argued with one of his daughters and condemned her to be executed. But he had no wish to meet her in the afterlife, so he had a hand cut off from her body.

There is a story that the mummified hand was taken to England in 1890 by Count Louis Hamon. His wife hated it – and she hated the story of the poor girl – so Louis locked the hand in a safe at his London home.

In October 1922, he opened the safe and was horrified to see the hand had changed. After 3,000 years as a mummy it was now soft flesh again. On the Halloween night of 31 October 1922, Hamon laid the hand gently in the fireplace and read aloud a prayer from the Egyptian Book of the Dead.

As he closed the book there was a lightning strike that plunged the house into darkness. The door was thrown open by a sudden chill wind and the couple were thrown to the floor.

Looking up they saw the ghostly and ghastly form of a woman. She was wearing the royal clothes of old Egypt and her right arm ended in a stump.
The ghost bent over the fire and then vanished. The hand disappeared with her.

Four days later, Hamon learned that his friend Lord Carnarvon had discovered King Tutankhamun's tomb. Hamon wrote to him…

I know now that the Egyptians had powers which we do not understand. In the name of God, I ask you to take care.

Carnarvon never got that letter. He had entered King Tut's tomb and died soon after from a mosquito bite. The story says all the members of his expedition died soon afterwards, killed by the 'Curse of the Mummy's Tomb'.

Great story. But Count Louis Hamon was a fortune teller and the ghost story added to his mystery. It made him rich and famous.

'Curse of the Mummy's Tomb'? Codswallop of the Mummy's Tomb, more like.

ROTTEN ROMAN PHANTOM

BUY YOUR DREAM VILLA

GHOSTS-WITH-THE-MOSTS
ESTATE AGENTS

THOSE PESKY OWNERS WON'T SELL?

Call GHOSTS-WITH-THE-MOSTS.

They'll kill to get rid of their property when we supply:

GHOSTS, GHOULS, PHANTOMS AND SPOOKS

Contact us now at ghosts-with-the-mosts.rome

One of the first ghost stories to be written was in Roman times. Pliny was a Roman lawyer who lived from AD 63 to AD 113. He wrote lots of letters to Roman emperors, friends and people he worked with. The letters can still be read today.

One letter told of the famous day when the Mount Vesuvius volcano erupted and began to swallow the city of Pompeii. Pliny's uncle was one of the people who died there. His uncle sailed to Pompeii to rescue some friends. But his ship was trapped. Pliny said…

> *Ash was now falling on the ships. It grew darker and denser the closer my uncle's ship went. Dust fell along with rock that was black and burnt and broken by fire. The sea was becoming clogged and ash from the volcano was blocking the shore. My uncle paused for a moment, wondering whether to turn back.*
>
> *Pliny*

His uncle didn't turn back and was trapped. He waited for the wind to change and blow his ship back out to the safety of the sea. It didn't, so he set off on foot through the hot and smoky air. His friends later reported that he sat down and could not get up. He was left behind.

When they went back three days later, they found he had turned to stone under hardened ash.

Pliny the storyteller tried to flee by coach, but the roads were blocked by people. He got out and ran and lived.

Pliny also talked about some of the fantastic feasts the rich people in Rome would eat. All the food in this story was eaten at some time in Rome – even parrot heads and pheasant tongues, hares with wings and roast boar filled with singing birds.

One of Pliny's most famous stories is the one about the ghost in the garden. It is one of the world's first ever ghost stories.

Pliny was a clever man and he believed it.

Dear Licinius Sura,

I promised you a ghost story and this is a true story from Greece that I once heard.

In Athens there was a large house. People said strange noises could be heard at night, like iron clanking on iron. Maybe rattling chains. At first the sound seemed to be far away, but if you waited it came closer and closer. Then there would appear the ghost in the shape of an old man, skinny and filthy with long hair and beard.

The family in the house could not bear the scary sounds and left it to the ghost. After some time, the owners decided to sell the house, but very cheaply.

Once, Athenodorus – a teacher – visited Athens. He heard about the house and decided he had to buy it. When night came, Athenodorus sat outside the front of the house. After a while he heard the chains rattling. The teacher read a book and pretended he wasn't interested. But the sounds did not stop.

At last, Athenodorus looked up and saw the ghost. It looked at him and began to beckon. The teacher got up, picked up an oil lamp and followed the ghost into the yard. Suddenly it disappeared. Athenodorus marked the spot where he last saw the ghost.

The next day, the owner asked the local people to dig in the market place outside the haunted house. There they found the buried skeleton of a man. He had been bound by chains and had marks of torture. The skeleton was given a proper burial.

The house in Athens was never haunted again.

MANY GHOST STORIES HAVE HAD THE SAME IDEA...

1. SOMEONE DIES HORRIBLY
2. THEIR SPIRIT CANNOT REST
3. THE REMAINS ARE LAID TO REST AND THE GHOST NEVER RETURNS

We can be sure most Romans would have believed Pliny's famous ghost story. Do you?

CUT-THROAT CELT CREEPINESS

The Romans ruled over the Celts in Gaul (France) and in Germany and then invaded Britain. The Celts had their own terrible tales of life after death.

52 BC Caesar and his Romans defeat the Celts in Europe and rule France. The Celts start looking across the English Channel to Britain.

AD 43 Emperor Claudius defeats the Celts in Britain. They're driven back to the hills of Wales and Scotland.

AD 61 A very bloody rebellion led by Queen Boudicca ends in another win for the Romans.

AD 312 Emperor Constantine becomes a Christian and the

Roman Empire converts to Christianity. Even the Celts are converted, and their old ways die. No more sacrifices.

The old Celts had priests called Druids to look after their afterlife. The Romans said the Druids were cruel and bloodthirsty.

A Celtic legend said the dead could be deadly.

> **O**ne Halloween a young man called Nera took on a challenge. There were two corpses hanging from a gallows on the hilltop. Nera agreed to tie a grass rope round the foot of one corpse for a bet. But as soon as the rope touched the foot Nera vanished into the Otherworld, and some legends say he was never seen in this world again.

Phantom fiction?

HORRIBLE HALLOWEEN

HALLOWEEN. EVERY YEAR, ON 31 OCTOBER, PEOPLE PRETEND TO BE DEAD. THEY DRESS UP AS SKELETONS, ZOMBIES, DEMONS OR WITCHES TO TRY TO SCARE PEOPLE

DO THEY EVER DRESS UP AS TEACHERS?

NAH. *FAR* TOO SCARY

On Halloween these days children (and daft adults) try to scare the people in their street by knocking on their doors after dark.

This annoying habit is called Halloween. That's a 'hallow' (or 'holy') 'een' (or 'evening'). Halloween = Holy Evening.

Imagine the world we live in and a world where the dead live. In between there is a magical curtain. People and ghosts can't see through or pass through. Halloween is the night when that curtain is really thin, and the living can see the spirits of the dead. It's the evening when ghosts pop back to visit their homes.

You are SUPPOSED to see human ghosts. You are NOT supposed to see any of the creatures that people dress up in now. The most popular in the 2020s were...

WITCH
RABBIT
DINOSAUR
SPIDER-MAN
FAIRY
CLOWN

Thousands of children annoy their town by dressing up and saying, 'Give me a treat or I'll do something nasty to you.'

If you did this at any other time of the year you would be arrested. When a police officer grabs you by the collar and says, 'Hallow, hallow, hallow,' then tell them these facts about Halloween...

HALLOWEEN FACT FILE

1 Halloween is also known as All Saints' Eve, and it is when devils are said to be at their most dangerous and powerful.

2 Halloween celebrations are an ancient idea. The Celtic people of Ancient Britain held a feast to celebrate the end of summer. The Romans said that the British priests (the Druids) made human sacrifices to the gods at the celebration.

3 The Romans said the Druid sacrifices were made by fastening live prisoners and animals in a huge wooden cage then setting fire to it. The Romans were probably lying about the frying.

24

4 The Romans celebrated their Day of the Dead on 21 February but Pope Boniface changed it to All Saints' Day and made it 13 May. A later pope, Gregory III, changed it again to 1 November.

5 Halloween lanterns are a reminder of an old legend about an Irishman called Jack. Jack upset the Devil and the Devil threw a piece of coal from Hell at him. Jack caught the hot cinder in a hollow turnip. But it didn't do him much good. Jack-o'-Lantern is doomed to wander the earth showing his light till the end of time.

By the time you've told the police officer all this they will be asleep, so you can escape the handcuffs. But BEWARE. That does not mean you are safe.

DID YOU KNOW...

In the 1990s a Chinese woman who moved to Britain had never heard of Halloween or the 'trick or treat' game. She really believed there was a ghost at her door. She threw a pan of boiling water over an eight-year-old boy. Only his mask and bin-liner costume saved him from serious injury. The poor woman was ordered to pay the boy £750 for the scalds he received.

Some trick – some treat.

SAINTS ALIVE

After about AD 300 most Celts became Christian and stopped blood sacrifices. But the idea of ghosts and an afterlife went on. Some Christians died horribly, and their spirits did miracles AFTER they were dead. These people became 'saints'. People like Winifred…

SAINT WINIFRED THE WET

In Wales in the 600s, the young Prince Caradoc loved Winifred, but she made it clear she did not want to marry him. She was a nun, married to God.

This upset the young prince so he drew his sword and cut off her head – as princes sometimes do when you upset them. As her head hit the ground there wasn't so much a splat as a splash. Because a spring of water gushed out of the dry rock.

Along came Winifred's uncle, a saint called Beuno. He stuck her head back on her body and she came back to life. (She had just a thin white line round her neck to show where she'd had her little accident.)

Beuno was not so kind to Caradoc. The saint cursed the prince till the earth opened up and swallowed him. This taught him a lesson he'd never forget because he was dead before he could remember.

Even his family suffered from Beuno's curse. They barked like dogs until they made a pilgrimage to the well to say sorry. They probably threw money down the well to keep Bueno happy. That would stop them feeling ruff.

Winifred's well waters are now said to cure sick people.

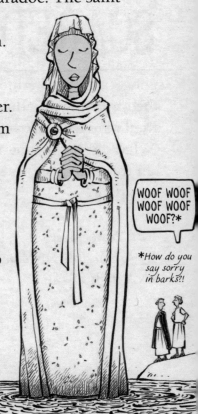

WOOF WOOF WOOF WOOF WOOF?*

*How do you say sorry in barks?!

The well is still visited by tourists. But Winifred's bones were carted off to Shrewsbury Abbey by a group of monks in 1137.

SCAREDY SCOTS

If you were a Celt you'd believe a dead person's ghost could rise from its coffin and haunt you. What did the northern Celts – the Scots – put on the dead person's stomach to stop their ghost escaping?

a) A horseshoe
b) A *Horrible Histories* book
c) A dish of salt

Answer:

(c) The salt also kept away the Devil. Friends of the dead person were expected to come and touch the corpse. If they didn't then they'd be haunted by its ghost. Children were also expected to touch the corpse. An extra treat was that it helped get rid of warts.

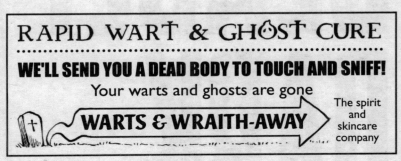

RAPID WART & GHOST CURE

WE'LL SEND YOU A DEAD BODY TO TOUCH AND SNIFF!

Your warts and ghosts are gone

WARTS & WRAITH-AWAY

The spirit and skincare company

DEADLY DARK AGES

SAXON TIMELINE

410 The Romans leave Britain but the Angles, Saxons and Jutes rush in and settle before the free Celts can get back. A bit like musical chairs.

493 The British Celts make one last effort to drive out the Saxons and win the Battle of Badon. Their leader is the awesome King Arthur ... maybe.

793 The Vikings are coming. Bad news for savaged Saxons and massacred monks. These are just raids – later they'll be back to stay.

871 Alfred the Great becomes king of Wessex and defeats and drives back the vicious Vikings from the south of England. But they don't go home. They stay in the north and the east.

1066 And that's that. The last Saxon king, Harold, is defeated by William the Conqueror and his Normans.

DID YOU KNOW...

POWERFUL POLTERGEISTS

A wicked spirit that can throw objects around is called a poltergeist. It can disturb a household by moving things as well as making banging or rapping sounds.

The first poltergeist was reported in 856 at a farmhouse in Saxon Germany. The poltergeist tormented the family living there by throwing stones and starting fires, among other things.

HAUNTING HEROES

King Arthur – the last of the Ancient British heroes – died in 537.

And he didn't. Some say he is just sleeping along with his knights.

YES, BUT IT'S NEARLY FIFTEEN HUNDRED YEARS AGO!

IT'S WHAT YOU CALL A GOOD 'KNIGHT'S' SLEEP, HEH–HEH

AND THEY SAY MY JOKES ARE BAD

An old English writer, Thomas Mallory, wrote…

> **Y**et some men say in many parts of England that King Arthur is not dead, but in another place; and men say that he shall come again.

The legend says that if Britain is threatened by the forces of dark and evil, Arthur and his knights will rise from their sleep and lead the country to safety.

Britain was attacked many times through the centuries. In the 1800s a French emperor, Napoleon, was a terrible danger. But he was beaten at the famous Battle of Waterloo by the Duke of Wellington.

The legend says Arthur and his army are sleeping underground until they are needed. There is a cave in Herefordshire called King Arthur's Cave.

The skeleton of a 'giant human' was discovered in the cave around 1700. A doctor called Pye collected the bones. Was it King Arthur's skeleton?

He then set off on a ship to Jamaica and took the huge skeleton with him. Perhaps the ghost of Arthur cursed Doc Pye for moving him? Anyway, the ship sank and the skeleton was lost.

DRAKE'S DRUM

King Arthur isn't the only haunting hero waiting to come back. In 1596 Sir Francis Drake died. He was a slave trader and pirate who helped to defeat the Spanish Armada in 1588. But just before he died, he ordered the ship's drum to be taken to his home at Buckland Abbey in Devon, England. He said that if England was ever in danger – and someone was to beat the drum – he would come back to defend the country. (Some people say the drum beats itself when the country is in danger.)

A famous poem by Henry Newbolt imagined the dying duck … I mean Drake…

> *Take my drum to England, hang it by the shore,*
> *Strike it when your powder's running low;*
> *If enemies sight Devon, I'll quit the port of Heaven,*
> *And drum them up the Channel as we drummed*
> *them long ago.*

Great. At last a USEFUL ghost.

They say the drum was heard in 1914 when the First World War began. And in 1918, when the German navy surrendered at the end of the war, drumming was heard on HMS *Royal Oak*. The ship was searched but no drum nor a drummer was found on board. They believed it was Drake's drum.

SLAVE SERVANT

Drake's slave trading helped make many British people rich. It was pure misery for the victims – the slaves. They could dream of being free and going home AFTER they died. That dream didn't always come true.

An old servant at Bettiscombe Manor in Dorset

begged his owner, Azariah Pinney, to send his body home to the West Indies. Pinney ignored the old man's dying wish and had him buried in a local graveyard.

The dead servant's ghost haunted the manor until the Pinney family had his skeleton dug up and taken back to the manor. The haunting stopped. It wasn't the West Indies, but the ghost seemed happy enough in the house.

In time the bones were lost, all except the skull. If anyone moves or disturbs the skull now they will hear it scream.

A true ghost story? No. In 1963 the skull was tested. It was three to four thousand years old. And it belonged to a young woman.

SKULL TEST®

DON'T BE CAUGHT OUT BY FAKE BONES

BUT DARLING, THEY SAID IT WAS AUTHENTIC

SOB

HOW COULD YOU?

DID YOU KNOW...

Slaves were worth a lot of money, but the traders didn't take very good care of them. Many enslaved people died as they were carried over the oceans. They were packed into dark, stinking rooms below the decks of the ships. A young slave described the journey of between forty and seventy days across the Atlantic Ocean…

The stench and the heat were dreadful. The crowding meant you hardly had room to turn over. The chains rubbed some Africans raw. The filth was made worse by the lavatory bucket and many small children fell into it. One day two of my countrymen were allowed on deck. They were chained together and decided they would rather have death than a life of such misery. They jumped into the sea.

WE'D RATHER BE GHOSTS

SAVAGED SAXON

Henry VIII's wife, Anne Boleyn, was beheaded. It's said her lips were still moving after her head hit the floor. Some doctors say it may be possible, but she couldn't speak because that needs breath from the lungs.

Yet one spooky story from Saxon times says a true hero can chat after they're chopped.

The Vikings were vicious. In 869 they invaded East Anglia and killed the Saxon king Edmund.

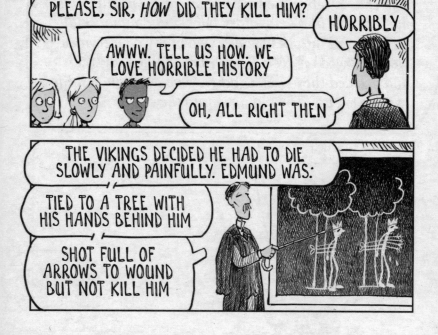

PLEASE, SIR, *HOW* DID THEY KILL HIM?

HORRIBLY

AWWW. TELL US HOW. WE LOVE HORRIBLE HISTORY

OH, ALL RIGHT THEN

THE VIKINGS DECIDED HE HAD TO DIE SLOWLY AND PAINFULLY. EDMUND WAS:

TIED TO A TREE WITH HIS HANDS BEHIND HIM

SHOT FULL OF ARROWS TO WOUND BUT NOT KILL HIM

This is what the Vikings called the 'Blood Eagle' because the spread lungs looked like eagle wings.

'But,' you cry, 'this is a *Horrible Histories* book of ghosts. That's a horror story, not a ghost story.'

'Hang on,' I cry back. I'm getting to the spooky bit.

The Saxons found the body of their king … but not his head. The Vikings had thrown it into a forest…

The Saxons searched and searched. Then they searched a bit more. No noble noddle. Then they heard a cry. 'Help me, help me.'

It was dead Ed's dead head. (Try saying that ten times quickly.)

The Saxons said this proved King Edmund was a saint. His body and his head were buried together.

MEASLY
MIDDLE AGES

MIDDLE AGES TIMELINE

1066 The Normans rule and they are ruthless.

1348 A plague known as the Black Death comes to Britain. Half of the people in the country catch it and die…

...YOU COULD SAY THEY'RE DYING TO MEET ME

1453 The Hundred Years War between England and France ends. French heroine Joan of Arc has been burned alive as a witch, but they still win.

LOSERS!

1483 King Richard III comes to the throne. His nephew, Edward, should have been king, but he disappears in the deadly Tower of London. Richard III won't last much longer…

LITTLE EDWARD IS DEADWARD SO I'M CLINGING TO KINGING

IN THE MIDDLE AGES, BEFORE STREET LIGHTING THE WORLD WENT VERY DARK AFTER SUNSET. ALL SORT OF FEARS WALKED THE STREETS AND FIELDS

I BET PEOPLE THOUGHT THERE WERE EVIL GHOSTLY SPIRITS OUT THERE, JUST WAITING TO GET THEM

THEY MUST HAVE BEEN SCARED

YES, BUT THEY HAD WAYS OF DEALING WITH GHOSTS...

GET THAT GHOST

SCARED OF GHOSTS? HERE ARE OUR TOP TIPS FOR ENDING THE EVIL SPIRITS

BROOMS

People of Eastern Europe put a broom under their pillow to keep away evil spirits while they sleep. English people like to place the broom across the doorstep of the house.

CANDLES

The light from a candle will keep bad spirits away from your dying friends. They should also be left burning for a week after their death so devils can't snatch their spirits. The Irish custom is to circle the dead body with twelve candles.

CAIRNS

Piles of stones over a grave are called a cairn. They not only protect the dead from having their graves robbed, but their weight also prevents the dead rising from their graves to haunt the living.

SALT

Carrying salt in your pocket or scattering it across your doorstep will keep ghosts away. Throw a little salt over your left shoulder and it will bring good luck.

IRON

Iron is a powerful defence against ghosts, witches and other evil spirits. An iron horse-shoe hung on a stable door will protect a house or stable. Iron nails taken

40 PIECE CAIRN KIT!

from a coffin will stop you having nightmares if you drive them into your bedroom door. An iron bar across a grave will stop a ghost rising from the grave.

SILVER

Most people know the legend of silver bullets killing werewolves. The metal is also a defence against ghosts, especially if made into the shape of a silver cross.

CROSSES

If you're unfortunate enough to meet one, then making the sign of the cross in the air will protect you against an evil ghost.

PRAYERS

Christians believe that saying the Lord's Prayer will protect you against ghosts. But beware – saying the same prayer backwards is a way of raising the Devil.

TWISTED TALES

The Middle Ages brought printed books. Now ghost stories could be written down and passed around. Some of the stories carried top tips to stop hauntings. Stories like:

THE DEAD BAKER WHO THROWS ROCKS

In the 1400s a baker died. But he kept coming back to life. And he was a nuisance. He went back to his kitchen and tried to help his family make the bread for the village.

He scared the family off, so the villagers were short of bread.

The villagers drove the baker's ghost away, but it just kept coming back.

The ghost even threw rocks at the villagers … either rocks or rock cakes.

Then they noticed the ghost's legs were covered in mud up to the knees. A group went to the baker's grave and dug up his corpse. Surprise. His corpse had the same muddy marks up its legs.

The villagers tried weighing his body down to keep him in the grave. That didn't work.

In the end they broke the corpse's legs. That worked: he was never seen again.

Now you know what to do if you are haunted by a baker. Flour power.

SAVAGE SAINT

Religion and ghosts often went together for people in the Middle Ages. Cuthbert was a great saint associated with lots of miracles. But he didn't like women.

He was buried in Durham, and a law was passed that said women weren't allowed to set foot in the graveyard around the church, never mind the church itself. A Durham woman called Sungeova was returning home one evening from a night out with her husband. She never stopped complaining about the road. 'It's full of potholes and puddles,' she moaned. 'I can't keep my skirts clean.'

So she decided that they should take a shortcut through the churchyard of Durham Cathedral – even though women were banned. As she entered she was gripped with some kind of invisible horror. She screamed out, 'I'm losing my mind!'

Her husband grumbled, 'Come on, woman. There's nothing to be afraid of.'

But as soon as she staggered outside the hedge that surrounded the cemetery, she fell down.

Friends helped her husband to carry her home … but Sungeova was dead. Cruel Cuthbert's curse?

TUDOR TERROR

TUDOR TIMELINE

1485 King Richard III is beaten in battle by Henry Tudor. Henry is crowned Henry VII. The first of the terrifying Tudors.

1509 The monstrous Henry VIII comes to the throne and will lop off the heads off two wives. He brings the Protestant religion to England and starts executing Catholics.

I'M MAKING GHOSTS OUT OF CATHOLICS

AND WIVES

1553 Henry's daughter Mary is a Catholic and starts burning Protestants.

I'M MAKING GHOSTS OUT OF PROTESTANTS

1558 Henry's second daughter, Elizabeth I, takes over. She is a Protestant and starts executing Catholics. She even executes her cousin – Mary Queen of Scots.

I'M MAKING GHOSTS OUT OF CATHOLICS – AGAIN

AND ME!

1588 The Spanish send a huge fleet of ships – the Armada – to replace Elizabeth with a Catholic ruler. Sir Francis Drake helps to defeat the invasion.

IT'S ALWAYS ABOUT DRAKE! I HELPED TOO, BERT SCRUBBINS, BUT I DON'T GET MENTIONED IN ANY HISTORY BOOKS

EXCEPT THIS ONE

RESTLESS GHOSTS

Some lucky ghosts know exactly how long they are doomed to haunt the place where they died. Spooks like the Cold Lad of Hylton.

In the last days of Queen Elizabeth, little Roger Skelton, the Cold Lad, worked in the stables for Lord Hylton (near Sunderland in north-east England). One day his lordship ordered Roger to get his horse ready for hunting. But young Roger fell asleep.

His lordship had a fit of rage and struck the boy, killing him instantly. Well ... Hylton would normally have been hanged for that in those days. His lordship tried to dump the corpse in the castle pond.

That'll be why the lad got so cold. After a while the body floated to the surface and was dragged out. His lordship was accused and sent for trial. If he was found guilty then Roger would be avenged, and his spirit could rest in peace. But Hylton was a LORD. And so was his mate, the judge, Lord Durham. A fair trial? No chance.

The Spirit of Justice

Lord Durhan   Lord Hylton   Maid

DURHAM: Robert de Hylton, my old friend. How are you, old chap?

HYLTON: Not bad, old fellow. Just need to clear up this silly accidental death and then everything will be tickety-boo.

DURHAM: So, let's see the charge. You are charged that on the ninth of September you did slay this stable boy ... What's his name? Skeleton?

MAID: Skelton, sir.

DURHAM: Are you a witness?

MAID: I'm the jury, sir.

DURHAM: In that case, shut up. How do you plead, Hylton?

HYLTON: Not guilty, my old fruit.

DURHAM: You didn't murder him, Bob?

HYLTON: Of course not, old bean.

MAID: He did. His lordship's whip handle was covered in blood.

DURHAM: Silence in court. How did the blood get on the whip handle?

HYLTON: Glad you asked me that. The lad whatsisname ... Skeleton ... was asleep, so I gave him a little tap on the old noddle to wake him up. Must have had a thin skull, poor little chap. Died. Never felt a thing.

MAID: They heard the screams down in the kitchens.

DURHAM: Silence in court.

MAID: So how did Roger's body end up in the pond?

HYLTON: I tried to carry him to a doctor. Slipped and dropped him.

DURHAM: Sounds fair enough to me, my old friend. So, member of the jury, how do you find the defendant? Guilty or not guilty?

MAID: Guilty.

DURHAM: ...is the WRONG answer. Try again?

MAID: Not guilty?

DURHAM: A sensible verdict. Case dismissed. You're free to go, Bob. Come to my castle for dinner next Monday?

So, Roger did not get justice. He was doomed to wander round Hylton Castle wailing about being cold from his being dumped in the pond. The Cold Lad of Hylton was heard crying about the length of time that he had to wait for someone to 'lay' – or release – his ghost.

Woe is me, woe is me,

The acorn's not fallen from the tree,

That will grow the wood,

That will make the cradle,

That will rock the babe,

That will grow to the man,

That will lay me.

That's around a hundred years – 75 years for the oak to grow and 25 for the babe to grow.

The story of Lord Hylton killing his stable boy could be true. Roger Skelton died around 1600, so even if the story of his ghost were true, his ghost is at rest now.

And the lesson from history…?

HORRIBLE HAUNTS

FAMOUS PHANTOMS FACT FILE

Common people are NOT usually seen haunting a place for hundreds of years after they die. Common people like you or me … but especially you. Yet there are many famous people seen. People like:

Singers (Elvis Presley, whose wife chats to his ghost from time to time)

Actors (Marilyn Monroe – seen in as many places as Anne Boleyn)

Film-makers (Walt Disney – seen on the train at his Disneyland Railroad)

Magicians (Harry Houdini died on Halloween and is seen at his old house)

Presidents (Like Abraham Lincoln, who was shot while watching a play – and never got to see the end. Maybe that's why his ghost returns?)

Peasants like you, dear reader, have no chance. If you want to be a ghost, be a celebrity. OR die in a famous place.

Anne Boleyn was both.

Little Anne was married to the wicked King Henry VIII. She was his second wife. When Anne upset the king, he decided to have her head cut off. He SAID...

The truth is Henry wanted a son to take the throne when he died. Instead, Anne Boleyn gave birth to a daughter ... who grew up to be Queen Elizabeth I. Henry was furious and was already chasing after wife number three. Anne had to die.

He didn't want Anne to suffer with a clumsy axe taking a dozen chops to cut her head off. (That's what had happened to the Countess of Pole.)

The cruel king hired an expert French swordsman to take her head off with one stroke as she knelt and prayed.

Anne's ghost was then said to be seen in more places than any other ghost in the world.

THEY SAY SHE OFTEN APPEARS ON 19 MAY BECAUSE THAT WAS THE DATE WHEN SHE DIED IN 1536

IMAGINE THAT. A GHOST THAT OWNS A CALENDAR

People say they have seen her at...

• Blickling Hall, Norfolk, her family home

• Hampton Court, where Henry spent a lot of his time

• Hever Castle, where she grew up

• Rochford Hall in Essex, where King Henry VIII first saw young Anne Boleyn

• ...and in the Bloody Tower at the Tower of London, where she was executed.

The story of Blickling Hall in Norfolk says Anne was seen with her own head in her lap, riding in a phantom carriage, drawn by a headless coachman and four headless horses. Dangerous.

In the days of Queen Victoria (who reigned from 1837 to 1901) there were comic songs performed that made fun of sad Anne's execution.

Sometimes old King Henry gives a spread,
For all his pals and gals and ghostly crew.
The headsman carves the beef and cuts the bread,
Then in comes Anne Boleyn to spoil the do.
She holds her head up with a wild war whoop,
And Henry cries, 'Don't drop it in the soup.'
With her head tucked underneath her arm,
She walks the bloody tower,
With her head tucked underneath her arm,
At the midnight hour.

You wouldn't make fun of someone dying so horribly, would you? The Victorian singers did.

AWESOME APPARITIONS

HOW CAN YOU SEE A GHOST IF THERE'S NOTHING THERE?

YOU SEE WHAT IS CALLED AN 'APPARITION'. PEOPLE HAVE TRIED TO EXPLAIN IT

The idea is like a photo you can see long after a person died. Maybe nature has some way of 'recording' the images of someone's life and 'replaying' them. The replay can happen at a certain place at certain times to certain people. Just like a photograph, an apparition can be seen by the living – but of course the photo (or the apparition) cannot see the viewer.

IMAGINE THAT, A PICTURE THAT LOOKS BACK AT YOU.

YES, YOU!

BOOK NOW
APPARITION PHOTOGRAPHY STUDIO

PHANTOM FUN

Down the years hundreds of writers have told or shown ghost stories. In the days of Anne Boleyn's daughter, Elizabeth I, a playwright called William Shakespeare used ghosts to tell his stories in the early 1600s. In the play *Hamlet* the ghost of a dead king appears at a castle and speaks to his son.

In other words, the ghostly old king was murdered by the new king. Hamlet's dad wants revenge. He wants his son, Hamlet, to kill the new king. Does Hamlet obey? He does.

Does Hamlet kill the king? He does … but ends up dead himself. NOT a happy ending. Let that be a lesson to you. Never do what a ghost tells you.

In *Macbeth*, another play by Shakespeare, the Scottish king Macbeth murders the old king and is haunted by a long line of ghosts. Eight Scottish kings appear.

Also, the ghost of a murder victim, Banquo, turns up at a feast to haunt Macbeth (who ordered his murder).

BUT many people believe it is WRONG to show ghosts on stage.

Even today actors in other plays won't say the name Macbeth in the theatre or say any of the lines of verse from the play. It will bring them bad luck.

DID YOU KNOW...

Macbeth was written in 1606, so the curse struck early. On 7 August 1606 it is said that Hal Berridge, the boy-actor playing Lady Macbeth, died backstage during the performance.

PROFESSOR PEPPER

COULD THIS SHAKESPEARE BLOKE MAKE A GHOST APPEAR?

MAYBE HE COULD

COR, MR PIMM. SHOW US HOW

HE PROBABLY USED A TRICK CALLED PEPPER'S GHOST. HERE'S HOW IT WORKS

YOU PLACE A SHEET OF GLASS ACROSS THE STAGE AT AN ANGLE, THEN HIDE AN ACTOR AND SHINE A LIGHT ON THEM. THE AUDIENCE SEES THE REFLECTION ... LIKE A GHOST

ACTOR

LIGHT

SHEET OF GLASS

REFLECTION

STAGE

AUDIENCE

Professor Pepper said he invented the trick in 1862. Theatres all rushed to play the ghost show and they were very popular.

Thousands of people made thousands of pounds for Professor Pepper. For thirty years dozens of plays toured around the world using Pepper's Ghost. They told stories like Charles Dickens' *A Christmas Carol* with its three ghosts of Christmas plus Marley's ghost rattling chains … just like Hamlet's father 250 years before.

There was even a song about the trick:

> In music halls and theatres too,
> This Pepper's Ghost they show.
> The truly spooky trick to view,
> Some thousands each night go.

Pepper made the money, but YOU know he didn't really invent the ghost trick – it had been a man from Portugal called della Porta in 1580. By the 1860s Porta was too dead to argue, 'Hey, you pinched my idea.'

Two hundred and fifty years after Shakespeare died, Queen Victoria saw these proper Pepper wonders on the stages:

- Floating head of an executed criminal
- Little angels
- Skeletons
- Fountains and fireworks.

SLIMY STUART SPIRITS

SLIMY STUART TIMELINE

1603 Scottish king James I takes over the English throne when Elizabeth dies. He promises to be kind to Catholics but isn't so two years later…

1605 Guy Fawkes joins a Catholic plot to blow up James in Parliament but fails.

1625 Charles I comes to the throne but falls out with Parliament. His Cavalier soldiers go to war with Cromwell's Roundheads. Charles loses the war then loses his head.

1688 New king James II turns out to be a secret Catholic so he has to go in the Glorious Revolution.

1714 Queen Anne dies. The last of the slimy Stuarts slips away.

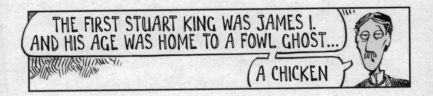

THE FIRST STUART KING WAS JAMES I. AND HIS AGE WAS HOME TO A FOWL GHOST...

A CHICKEN

THE STUFFED CHICKEN'S REVENGE

Francis Bacon was a great minister in the days of James I. (No pig jokes about his name, please.)

He turned his great brain to solving the problems of the world. Problems like, how do you stop food going bad? No, he didn't invent the fridge. Nearly as good.

As he was riding through London one snowy March day, he noticed that the frozen grass in the tracks was as fresh as ever.

MAYBE THE COLD IS KEEPING THE GRASS FRESH. I WONDER IF IT WOULD PRESERVE MEAT THE SAME WAY?

He told the coachman to stop the carriage at the nearest farm. He jumped out and bought a chicken. The coachman was ordered to kill the chicken, to pluck out most of its feathers and to clean out its insides. This he did.

Sir Francis bent down and began stuffing the chicken full of snow. He then packed it into a sack full of snow. It worked.

But the cold was too much for 65-year-old Francis. He started shivering and collapsed in the snow.

A few days later he was dead as the chicken.

Deader than the chicken, in fact. For the chicken wasn't finished. It went on to haunt the place. Half-plucked, it runs and flaps and shivers around Pond Square in London. Someone tried to catch it during the Second World War, but it disappeared into a brick wall.

It was last seen in the 1970s.

But that's not the only Stuart ghost story...

CHOPPED CHARLIE

Charles was born in 1600 and was beheaded in 1649. He argued with the English Parliament, who didn't like his rule. He said he had been sent by God to rule and didn't need Parliament. After a long war – the English Civil War – he was defeated.

Charles was executed in London. He wore two shirts for the execution so he wouldn't shiver and look scared. Of course, his ghost has been seen far and wide – even in a pub in Newcastle 250 miles away from where Chopped Charlie lost his head.

But it has been seen most of all at Chavenage House. That house had been built in 1576, and in December 1648, a group of horsemen rode up to see the owner, Nathaniel Stephens, a member of Parliament. The riders wanted him to come to London to vote to cut off the king's head. After arguing all night, he agreed and Charles would die.

But Nathaniel Stephens's daughter, Abigail, was away that night. When she found what her father had done, she was furious.

Nathaniel fell sick. Charles was executed and Nathaniel died soon after. Who popped up at Nathaniel's funeral? The ghost of King Charles, of course. The servants said…

THE COACH BURST INTO FLAMES AS IT WENT THROUGH THE GATES

FLAMES OF HELL, THEY BE COS THAT'S WHERE CHARLES WAS TAKING HIM

Chavenage House also has a bed that floats across the room, a 'grey lady' and a monk's spectre praying in the chapel.

THE CIVIL SOLDIER SPOOKS

There were so many battles between Charles and Parliament that there were a lot of dead soldiers around. And a lot of ghost stories waiting to be told.

One of the Civil War battles was at Edgehill on 23 October 1642. Charles claimed that he'd won – but so did Parliament army leader, Oliver Cromwell. Cromwell's army had shaved heads and wore round helmets, so they were known as Roundheads.

Two months after the battle some farm workers near Edgehill moaned that they were disturbed at night by the charging of horses, the roar of cannons and the blowing of bugles. The villagers went to see what was happening … and they saw the Battle of Edgehill – again.

And again.

And again … and again. Ghosts seemed to be acting out the battle every weekend.

Charles sent some of his officers to report and they said they saw the battle too. Charles's friends had been there for the real battle and knew some of the ghostly soldiers. They saw Sir Edmund Verney, who had been holding the king's flag until his hand was cut off, still holding the flagpole.

The ghostly battle can still be seen every year on 23 October, it is said.

CHOPPED CHARLIE'S LAST CHANCE

Charles himself was visited by a ghost. He signed the order that let the Roundheads dead-head his friend – Lord Strafford. One night Strafford's ghost came to Charles in his bedroom. But he didn't want revenge. He just wanted to warn the king that if he went to war with Parliament he'd lose his head too.

Charles told his commander, Rupert, who said it was just a bad dream. But the dream was right.

THE TERROR OF TEDWORTH

One of Britain's most famous ghost stories happened in Stuart times. It concerns the Phantom Drummer of Tedworth.

Lawyer John Mompesson was visiting the town of Ludgershall in Wiltshire when he heard the deafening sound of a drum.

'What's that horrible racket?' he asked.

He was told, 'It's a beggar. He has a special licence to beg and to use that drum to attract attention.'

Mompesson didn't believe a beggar could have a licence to drum. The beggar, William Drury, was brought before Mompesson and showed his licence. It was a very clumsy forgery.

Drury went to prison but begged to be allowed to keep the drum. Mompesson refused. Drury escaped from the prison, while the drum was sent to Mompesson's house. For the next two years the house suffered terrible drumming noises.

NOT THE GHOST OF THE LIVING DRURY. BUT THE GHOST OF THE DRUM ITSELF

I'VE GOT A BROKEN DRUM. YOU CAN'T BEAT IT

Then the ghostly drum grew more violent...

• A bible was found burnt
• An unseen creature gnawed at the walls like a giant rat, purred like a cat and panted like a dog
• Coins in a man's pocket turned black

- Great staring eyes appeared in the darkness
- The spirit attacked the local blacksmith with a pair of tongs
- A horse died of terror in its stable
- Chamber pots full of pee and poo were emptied into the children's beds.

Drury said it was his witch powers that were cursing Mompesson. The beggar was tried for witchcraft and sentenced to be exiled overseas. The haunting of Mompesson's house stopped.

And Drummer Drury was lucky. Twenty years earlier he would have been burned at the stake as a witch.

DID YOU KNOW...

DEAD DRUMMERS

There are many tales of ghost drummers. Scottish storytellers are fond of them.

Cortachy Castle, Kirriemuir, Scotland

Cortachy Castle, where the Ogilvy family live to this day, once had its own drummer. His job was to beat his drum as a warning when attackers came in sight. But the attackers paid him to stay silent.

He was a traitor. The defenders punished him by throwing him from a tower. Now he plays the drum when one of the Ogilvy family is about to die.

BOOM BANG TAP TAP TAP

ONE OF US IS DOOMED!

I KNEW IT WAS A MISTAKE TO BUY ALICE A DRUM KIT

Edinburgh High Street

In the early 1800s someone found the entrance to a secret passage in Edinburgh Castle. A weakness if the castle were ever attacked. It was so narrow no man could climb down. So, the council sent a little drummer boy down – with his drum. They needed to know where the entrance was that would let in any attackers.

The drummer boy rattled his drum as he crept down the passage. The council kept their ears to the ground and followed the drumming down the High Street. But, when it reached the Tron Church, the drumming stopped. It never started again, and the boy never appeared. The council sealed up the castle end of the tunnel and it hasn't been found since. Still, on quiet nights, they say, you can still hear a faint drumming coming from under the High Street.

Believe that … if you want to.

SCREAMING SKULLS

Weird Wardley

WARDLEY HALL NEAR MANCHESTER SAYS IT HAS A SCREAMING SKULL. IT WILL SCREAM IF YOU TRY TO REMOVE IT

The skull at Wardley is supposed to be from a monk, Father Ambrose. On Easter Sunday 1641, he was arrested for preaching the Catholic faith. He was hanged, drawn and quartered at Lancaster Castle.

That meant he was hanged till he was half dead, taken down and split open so his guts could be thrown on a fire, then beheaded and his body cut into four pieces.

Father Ambrose's head was put on show at Manchester as a warning to others. The message?

KEEP YOUR HEAD SCREWED ON. CATHOLIC PRIESTS WILL BE EXECUTED

HE'S GONE UP IN THE WORLD

HE HOLDS AN ELEVATED POSITION

GONE TO A HIGHER PLACE

YOU HAVE TO LOOK UP TO HIM

But Francis Downes from Wardley Hall, a Catholic, rescued the skull and hid it in a secret place in the house. The skull was found a hundred years later by a servant, who threw it into the moat.

That night there was a terrible storm that shook the building. The owner had the moat drained and the skull was put back where it was found.

Since then Father Ambrose's skull has been buried, burned and smashed but it is always found outside the hall the next day, wearing a grin.

The story was probably told to show that you can kill a priest, but you can't kill the Catholic religion.

Restless Rovers

One of the most famous wanderers is the *Flying Dutchman*. The crew of a Dutch ship in the late 1700s committed a terrible crime.

The crew of the Dutch pirate ship were struck down by a terrible plague and they all died. BUT their ghosts were doomed to sail the seas and never land again. Even the ship was a ghost.

Nobody ever wrote about seeing the ghostly *Flying Dutchman*. They only said they knew the story that sailors told.

Life at sea on a slow sailing ship would be boring. So stories would be told to pass the time. Countless sailors from around the world, and through time, have all sworn that they've seen something they call the *Flying Dutchman*.

Sea Ghosts Fact File

1. A Dutch captain, Hendrik van der Decken, lived in the 1660s. Van der Decken was a greedy and ruthless man who set sail from Amsterdam on the *Flying Dutchman* to make his fortune in the East Indies. Countless sailors from around the world, and through time, have all sworn that they've seen the *Flying Dutchman* in the ocean. Can they all be wrong?

2. The *Lady Lovibond*. Britain has its own phantom ship. On 13 February 1748, the *Lady Lovibond* was sailing by the dangerous Goodwin Sands off the coast of Kent, England. Her captain, Simon Peel, was on honeymoon with his bride and several wedding guests. But a jealous sailor (who was also in love with the bride) killed Peel and steered the ship to disaster on the sands. On 13 February 1798, fifty years later to the day, a fishing boat spotted a ship of the *Lady Lovibond*'s description heading for the sands. They heard party sounds and women's voices. But when the ship hit the sands it broke up ... and vanished. The same vision was seen in 1848 and 1898. Ghost hunters were on the lookout in 1948 and 1998 but saw nothing in the mist. Perhaps it will be back in 2048?

3. The blazing ghost ship. America's '*Flying Dutchman*' is the *Palatine*. It arrived off the coast of Rhode Island packed with Dutch settlers in 1752. A storm drove it off course and washed the captain overboard. The ship was driven onto rocks and started to break up. Local fishermen rowed out and took the passengers to safety but began stripping the ship of its valuable cargo before it sank. To cover up their crime, they set the ship ablaze, but as they rowed home, they were horrified to see a woman come up on deck. She'd been hiding from the looters. Her screams carried across the water until the flames swallowed her. Over the centuries a blazing ship has been seen off the coast of New England.

4. The ghost under the sea. The First World War German submarine UB65 was cursed from the start.

Workmen building her died in accidents, then on her first voyage an officer was killed in an explosion. From then on, the ghost of the officer was seen on board. A new captain and crew were chosen who did not believe in ghosts. For a while the ghost did not appear. But when the new captain left UB65 the ghost returned. One sailor went mad with fear and before a test dive jumped overboard. Still the submarine survived enemy attacks until, near the end of the First World War, it mysteriously blew up, killing the entire crew. An accident? Or a ghost's revenge for his own death?

5. The leading light. Many people know the history rhyme about how Christopher Columbus found America:

> *In fourteen hundred and ninety-two,*
> *Columbus sailed the ocean blue.*

Not so many people remember that Columbus himself had a ghostly vision at sea. When the crew were getting seriously worried about ever seeing land again, Christopher Columbus himself said he saw a light in the sky. It was a 'guiding star' that would lead them to the new world. No one else saw the light; no one believed Columbus. The next day they saw land – they had reached the American continent.

True Ghost Ship Story

Many 'ghost' stories aren't ghostly at all. In the late 1920s, the schooner *Ernest Mills* sank in a storm off the coast of Carolina, USA. A few days later the 'ghost' of the schooner appeared to the horror of the local people.

Except it wasn't a ghost. The schooner had been carrying a cargo of salt when she sank. When the salt dissolved, the Ernest Mills bobbed up to the surface of the ocean again. Mystery solved.

SKULDUGGERY

S creaming skulls pop up all over the place.

The Burton Agnes Skull

Some corpses refuse to rest in peace. Look at the story of the Burton Agnes Skull, which is a lot like Pliny's Roman story – but around 1,700 years later.

Burton Agnes Hall – near Driffield in the East Riding of Yorkshire, England – was built in 1598, while Elizabeth I was on the throne. Three sisters of the Griffith family had it built.

Then … disaster. The youngest sister, Ann, was attacked near her home by robbers. They beat her after she refused to give them her mother's ring. Townspeople heard her cries, saved her, and took her home. But she died five days later. On her deathbed, she asked for her head to be buried in the family tomb next to the hall. Then the problems started.

• The family ignored her dying wish. She was buried in the churchyard.

• But the sisters began to hear noises throughout the house. Her sisters had her coffin dug up. The body had not rotted at all.

• They removed the head and buried it away from the body.

• Some stories say the head was even grinning.

• The head was taken back to Burton Agnes Hall. The noises stopped.

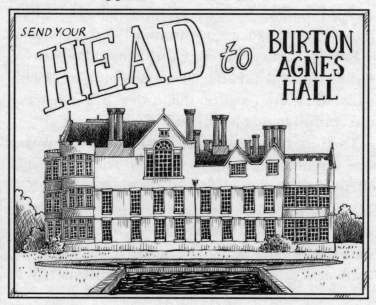

The Tunstead Farm Skull

The skull at Tunstead Farm, Derbyshire – they call it Dickie – knocks when a stranger comes near or when someone in the family is about to die. Who is Dickie? One story says it's a woman who was murdered by her sister, and that as she was dying she said she'd never rest. Another says it's a man who was thrown off the land his family owned.

The Calgarth Hall Skull

In the 1790s Myles Philipson, a Justice of the Peace, owned Calgarth Hall, Cumbria, England, and much land. He wanted more – he wanted the house of a young couple. The young couple refused to give up their home.

So, Philipson hid one of his silver cups in their home and told the police they had stolen it. They were hanged. As she stood on the scaffold the young wife cursed Philipson…

LISTEN HERE, MYLES PHILIPSON. THAT TINY LUMP OF LAND WILL BE THE DEAREST LAND A PHILIPSON HAS EVER BOUGHT. FOR YOU AND YOUR FAMILY WILL NEVER DO WELL ON IT. AND WHILE CALGARTH STANDS, WE'LL HAUNT IT DAY AND NIGHT.

Shortly after their execution, two skulls turned up in Calgarth Hall. They screamed loud every night. They were taken away but always came back. Philipson and his family became poor. In time the skulls were eventually boarded up in the walls of the house.

EXTREME PUNISHMENT FACT FILE

Screaming skulls? NOT true. But being hanged for stealing a silver cup? That could be TRUE.

There have been some horrible historical executions in the past … in the 1700s the law was terribly tough and hanged people for anything.

In the savage 1700s, 222 different crimes could be punished by hanging. If you stole something worth more than 5 shillings (25p) from a shop you could be hanged. Steal anything from a shipwreck? You're hanged. You could even be hanged if you were caught cutting down a tree or robbing a rabbit warren.

I WOULDN'T DO THAT IF I WERE YOU

But the punishment was so harsh this didn't work. The judge would look at the pathetic, poor and desperate criminal and decide…

I FIND THE ACCUSED NOT GUILTY

Judges and juries didn't want to see a criminal hanged for such a small offence, so they let them off. That meant the criminals were getting away with it. The law had to change.

From 1823 to 1837, a hundred of the hanging crimes were changed so the criminals went to prison instead.

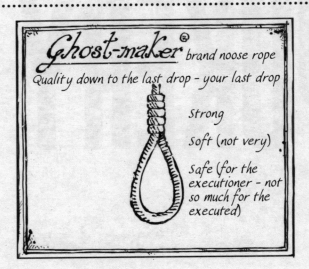

Ghost-maker ® brand noose rope

Quality down to the last drop – your last drop

Strong

Soft (not very)

Safe (for the executioner – not so much for the executed)

GEORGIAN JIGGERY-POKERY

GEORGIAN TIMELINE

1714 German Georges arrive to take over the throne of Britain for over a hundred years.

1745 Those Catholic Stuarts want their throne back. Bonnie Prince Charlie Stuart leads an invasion. In 1746 at the Battle of Culloden the Scots are massacred.

1776 Now the Americans are revolting. They beat the British and set up their own country, the United States of America.

THE COCK LANE LIARS

In 1762 George III – the third Georgian king – was on the throne. Posh ladies wore fine silk skirts and their hair was huge. It was padded out with all sorts of horrible stuff. A gentleman wrote a poem to warn the ladies that it could put men off…

When he sees your hair so thin,
Horsehair, rope and wool within.
When he scents the mingled steam,
Which your plastered heads are rich in,
Lard and meal and clotted cream,
Can he love a walking kitchen?

The rich men wore short and tight trousers, large wigs, delicate shoes, small hats and lots of scent. They were called macaroni.

The rich spent fortunes on silks and grand houses, while the poor were living in filth and hunger, dying young from diseases and hunger.

William Kent moved to 25 Cock Lane in London with his partner, Frances. He lived in a house owned by Richard Parsons. Kent loaned Parsons money. Parsons couldn't pay it back.

Then Frances died, and strange things happened in the shabby, crooked house in Cock Lane. Young Elizabeth Parsons, aged 12, said...

I SLEEP THERE, AND SINCE FRANCES DIED I'VE HEARD STRANGE SCRATCHING NOISES AT NIGHT

Her father, Richard Parsons, said...

IT IS THE GHOST OF FRANCES. SHE IS TRYING TO SEND US A MESSAGE

He called in a priest, and they were able to 'talk' to the dead woman. They asked the haunted room a question and the ghost knocked once for 'yes' and twice for 'no'.

AND THE MESSAGE IS THAT KENT POISONED HER WITH ARSENIC

Hundreds of people came to Cock Lane to see the ghost – or to hear it scratching and knocking. The Duke of York went along too. So many people rushed there that the lane was blocked.

They held a 'séance' – a meeting with dead spirits. The dead woman scratched and knocked. The famous writer Dr Johnson went along to a séance and the truth came out.

Young Elizabeth was seen creeping from her bed to pick up a small piece of wood that she used to make the scratching and knocking sounds.

I WOODEN DO SUCH A THING

Richard Parsons was put in a pillory and sent to jail for two years. The pillory was a cruel punishment.

THE PILLORY FACT FILE

The head and hands were held in a wooden frame and the victim had to stand. If they grew tired then the neck-hole could choke them. An old Newcastle woman almost died this way in 1758 – her crime was fortune-telling. In 1560 a London maid who tried to poison her mistress was placed in the pillory and had one of her ears cut off. Sometimes thousands of people gathered at the pillory – pickpockets had a wonderful time.

People liked to throw stuff at criminals in the pillory. Rotten fruit and vegetables were popular – but sometimes they threw the odd dead cat.

The stocks and pillory were banned in the UK after 1837.

The people of Smithfield treated Parsons kindly and didn't pelt him. They even collected money to help him pay off Kent. He was lucky.

The prison would have been dirty, crowded and full of the dreadful disease typhus. But at least he was alive.

William Kent was lucky too. If the law had said he was guilty of poisoning Frances he would have been executed. Crowds would have come to see him hang.

HANG AROUND FOR A PARTY

In London, prisoners were taken to chapel on the Sunday morning before they were hanged. They sat round their empty coffin while a priest told them how wicked they were.

Next day they were taken three miles in open carts to Tyburn (now Marble Arch), where large crowds gathered. It was like a street party – a good day out known as 'Tyburn Fair'. There was food and drink on sale and grandstand seats for a good view.

The bodies of executed criminals, especially highwaymen, were often hung in chains to rot at the scene of their crimes. A 'gibbet' used for this hanging is still on show at Caxton near Huntingdon. The hangings took place once a month.

A poet called John Taylor has written this dreadful

ditty about Tyburn gallows. He compares Tyburn victims to fruit hanging from a tree.

The Tyburn Tree, it does appear,
Has dangling fruit twelve times a year.
It has no leaf, no roots, no bud,
The rain that makes it grow is blood.

It, by the roadside, stands for years
Yet no one steals the fruit, I hear.
Like all bad fruit both far and wide
It's eaten by the worms inside.

DID YOU KNOW ...

GRAVE CRIMES

Some hanged criminals' bodies went to the doctors – not to be cured, but to be cut up for experiments.

Surgeons were allowed to practise on the dead bodies of criminals to see how the human body worked. A law of 1752 said any executed criminal could be used. Criminals could be brave about being hanged – but were terrified at the thought of being cut up after they were dead.

VICTORIAN VILLAINS

VICTORIAN TIMELINE

1837 Queen Victoria comes to the throne. A cruel age with children working down mines and factories, up chimneys to clean them for rich folk, and living in slums.

ROOF TOP   ALOOF TOFF

1843 Charles Dickens writes *A Christmas Carol*, one of the most popular ghost stories EVER.

1868 A new law says criminals can't be hanged in public – only behind the prison walls.

1888 Jack the Ripper stalks the streets of London killing women. He is never caught.

Those Victorians loved a good ghost story. They also loved a good murder story. So, the most popular story on stage was a ghostly murder story. And what made it most amazing was it was supposed to be TRUE. The murderer was William Corder, and the victim was Maria Marten. The place was the Red Barn on Corder's land at Polstead in Suffolk.

Corder was acted out on stage as an evil villain. Maria as a helpless maiden whose ghost returned to tell the world she'd been murdered. But if Corder could tell HIS side of the story, it may look different.

WILLIAM CORDER'S STORY

My song is sung on every street in Suffolk. You'll have seen the ballads they printed and sold for a penny. It told my tragic tale.

My name is William Corder, to you I do declare,
I courted Maria Marten, most beautiful and fair.
I promised I would marry her, upon a certain day,
Instead of that I was resolved to take her life away.
I then went home and fetched my gun, my pickaxe and my spade,
I went into the Red Barn, and there I dug her grave.
So, you young men that do pass by, with pity look on me,
For murdering Maria Marten, I'll be hanged upon the tree.

William Corder

Most of it is lies and I want to tell you my side of the story. Hanged upon a tree? They mean the 'gallows tree', of course. It stood outside Bury St Edmunds jail and thousands of people came from all over the county to watch me die. My death was slow and painful, so I hope they enjoyed their day out.

They hated me. They believed I killed the 'beautiful and fair' Maria. The harmless, helpless girl? That is a joke. A bitter, laugh-less joke. For a start, Maria was no child – she was two years older than I was.

Maria Marten

She'd had two babies before we met and then she had my baby. Of course, the law said that any woman with a baby had to name the father. He would be arrested and forced to marry her.

Maria said she was going tell the constable and she said I had to marry her ... or else face prison. I was the son of the squire. I lived in a fine house and would be a landowner. Marry Maria? Go to jail? Which was worse? Marry the filthy, peasant daughter of a molecatcher?

Then our baby died. Poor thing, I know, but lots of babies died young in our world. I thought that I was free of jail and free of Maria. But then she came to me and said that she was going to the law anyway. She would tell him I had given our baby poison and murdered it. I wouldn't go to jail – I would hang.

I offered her money. She said no. She wanted me to marry her. There was only one way out. I had to frighten her and make her give up her blackmail.

I made my plans. On my mother's land there was a large barn. On a clear evening it caught the red rays of the setting sun, so everyone called it the 'Red Barn'. I told Maria a lie, 'If we are going to marry, we shall have to run away together. Dress yourself as a man and meet me in the Red Barn at midnight.'

My plan was to get to the barn an hour before her. I took a pickaxe and a spade to dig a grave to frighten her. I would point a pistol at her and tell her to forget about marriage. I never meant to carry out my threat, I didn't.

On my way to the Red Barn that night I met Maria's stepmother, Mrs Anne Marten. Anne was not much older than Maria and there was no motherly love between them. She saw the pickaxe and the spade and knew my secret.

Maria arrived. 'Don't go to the constable or I'll kill you.' She laughed at my threats. Somehow the gun went off and she fell to the floor of the Red Barn, dead.

I buried her in the grave I'd dug. I went to London and told everyone Maria had run away with me. I paid Mrs Marten to keep quiet. More blackmail. But after a year I thought I was safe and stopped sending her money.

So, Anne Marten came up with a fantastical ghost story. She said Maria had appeared to her in a dream and told her I'd killed her and buried the body in the Red Barn.

They believed her ghost story. They dug in the Red Barn and found the corpse. They arrested me and after an unfair trial I was led to the gallows.

I was betrayed by a ghost. A ghost that never was.

The Red Barn

DID YOU KNOW...

Corder died on the end of the hangman's rope and a plaster mask was made of his face. His story was printed in a book. His body was skinned and used to cover a copy of the book. The book and the mask can be seen at Moyse's Hall Museum in Bury St Edmunds, not far from where he was hanged.

TERRIBLE TWENTIETH CENTURY

TWENTIETH CENTURY TIMELINE

1901 Queen Victoria dies. End of an age.

1914 The First World War starts. Britain and her friends against Germany and her friends. Millions die violently.

1939 The Second World War starts. Same again but far more die in blitzes and battles.

1993 *Horrible Histories* books are born. Lucky children everywhere can laugh and learn … and shiver and shudder.

THE ANGEL OF MONS

Whe people go to war, they like to think that their god is on their side. Ancient people made sacrifices to get their gods to bring them luck in battle.

In August 1914 British troops arrived in southern Belgium to try and stop the German invasion. They were beaten back and slaughtered by the advancing enemy. Over 15,000 died in the early attacks. Yet some survived. British and French soldiers said this was thanks to a ghostly miracle. But the British and the French saw a different miracle…

WE SAW OUR ST GEORGE LEADING A TROOP OF PHANTOM FIGHTERS ON HORSEBACK. THEY DROVE THE GERMANS BACK

OUI, MON AMI, BUT IT WAS OUR JOAN OF ARC, NOT ST GEORGE WHO CAME TO OUR RESCUE

C'EST BIEN, GEORGE, I'VE GOT THIS

Arthur Machen, a writer, turned the tale into a short story. His story (called 'The Bowmen') said it was the English heroes of the 1415 Battle of Agincourt who had come to the rescue. (The battle was fought nearby.)

Machen's story was published in the *London Evening News* a few weeks after the Battle of Mons and many Brits believed it. Some of the soldiers who returned from the battle then said it was true.

THEY WAS DIRTY GREAT ANGELS WITH ROBES AND WINGS AND THINGS

Even when Machen said he'd invented the whole story there were some people who went on believing in the angels.

Some religious people have said the phantom army was made up of the spirits of the soldiers who had just died in the battle.

Some doctors believed that the Allied soldiers had 'hallucinations' – waking dreams – because they were stressed by fear, pain and exhaustion.

But, weirdest of all, the German spy chief, Friedrich Herzenwirth, claimed it was a German angel and HE created it.

Horrible Histories note: we interviewed God about taking sides. She said, 'Piffle. I am not on the side of ANYONE who goes to war. Bless you and all who read your wonderful books.'

SPIRITUAL SPOOKS

It wasn't just German spies who faked ghostly visions. Spiritualists say you may speak to a dead loved one through a special living person – a medium.

In the Frightful First World War there were hundreds of thousands of dead – over 900,000 from British families alone.

There were people who talked to the dead written about in the Bible, 3,000 years ago. King Saul went to visit a spiritualist, the Witch of Endor, to see if he could talk to the old king, Samuel. The spirit of Samuel had bad news...

YOU AND YOUR THREE SONS WILL DIE IN TOMORROW'S BATTLE

OH GREAT. I REALLY DID NOT WANT TO HEAR THAT

WOEFUL WOMEN

The Fox sisters became really popular after the American Civil War (1861–65), when so many people died.

THE FOX FAMILY FACT FILE

A family called Fox lived near New York. There was farmer James Fox, his wife and two daughters, Maggie and Katie. In 1848 their house was disturbed by strange banging noises in the night. The girls discovered they could talk with a troubled spirit through rapping – one rap for 'yes', two raps for 'no'. Eventually they learned that the rappings came from the spirit of a man called Charles Rosma. Rosma told of how he was murdered and buried in the cellar. When neighbours helped the Fox family to dig in the cellar they found human hair and bones. The spirit said he was murdered by a Mr Bell, but that the killer would never be brought to justice. Mr Bell, who'd lived in the house five years before the Fox family, was very angry and denied it. But the case caused such a sensation in the newspapers that the Fox girls became famous and appeared all over America. The 'spiritualist' movement started in America and many people copied the performances of the Fox girls.

After forty years of fame Katie admitted it was all a trick … but the spiritualists refused to believe her. The Fox sisters had cleverly cracked their toe knuckles to fool their mother. They tricked their neighbours and then the rest of the world saying...

It is said they even fooled US president Abraham Lincoln. His wife, Mary Lincoln, was a great believer in speaking to spirits. A family of mediums, the Lauries, held the séances, and President Lincoln went along with his wife. A newspaper reported...

PIANO WALTZES AROUND THE ROOM

At a Laurie séance last night Mrs Miller played the piano. As she played the large piano began to rise and fall.

President Lincoln then placed his hand on the piano and pressed down but still the piano rose and fell a number of times when Mrs Miller asked it to.

The president, with a smile, said, 'I think we can hold down that instrument.' He then climbed upon it, sitting with his legs dangling over the side. So did Mr Somes, S. P. Kase, and a soldier in the army. Still the piano, with this enormous added weight, continued to wobble. The men were glad to climb down. Mr Lincoln said he was sure this was caused by some 'invisible power'.

After a while Mary Lincoln held her own séances. She wanted to speak to her son, Willie, who had died from typhoid fever. She held a séance in the home of the US presidents, the White House. She told a friend…

WILLIE LIVES. HE COMES TO ME EVERY NIGHT AND STANDS AT THE FOOT OF THE BED WITH THE SAME SWEET, ADORABLE SMILE THAT HE ALWAYS HAD. HE DOES NOT ALWAYS COME ALONE. SOMETIMES HIS DEAD BROTHER, LITTLE EDDIE, IS WITH HIM

President Abraham Lincoln was shot dead in 1865 by a war enemy. After he died, of course, his ghost began to pop up at the White House all the time. The British prime minister, Winston Churchill (1874–1965), said he'd seen the ghost.

FIRST WORLD WAR WOES

It wasn't just angels at Mons that made the First World War spooky.

By the end of the war in 1918 hundreds of thousands of people had lost their loved ones. Many turned to spiritualists to help them speak to dead sons, daughters, husbands and wives.

There were some clever people who argued that people could speak to the dead through a medium. One of them was Arthur Conan Doyle, who was famous for writing the Sherlock Holmes books. His son Kingsley died in the war and Arthur wanted to chat to him.

In 1919 he met the 'Masked Medium' – a woman who hid the bottom half of her face under a veil. She said she could call up the dead in a séance.

The Masked Medium made a ghost appear. Arthur was amazed. He did a tour round Britain and Australia to say…

Do you believe this famous and clever man? Or was he fooled? The Masked Medium was proved to be a fake.

In 1917 two girls in Yorkshire, Elsie and Frances, cut out some pictures of fairies from a book. They hung them from strings then took photos of themselves with the fake fairies floating in front of them. Arthur said…

In 1983 the girls – elderly women by now – said they had faked it.

GHOST BUSTERS
1. JAMES RANDI (1928–2020)

Many people have said ghosts and spiritualism are all fakes. A magician called James Randi spent his life showing how fakers worked using stage-magic tricks like Pepper's Ghost…

> IT'S A FAKE, A SCAM, A SWINDLE AND A FRAUD. IF ANYONE CAN PROVE THEY TALK TO SPIRITS, I WILL GIVE THEM A MILLION DOLLARS

No one passed his tests, and no one won the million dollars.

GHOST BUSTERS
2. HARRY HOUDINI (1874–1926)

Harry Houdini was a magician who was famous for escaping from impossible traps.

He was known as the 'Handcuff King'. But he never WANTED to be remembered for magic and escaping. He wanted to be remembered as the man who proved mediums were all fakes.

Harry showed that the famous American 'Witch of Lime Street' was a fraud. He hated the mediums who took money from unhappy people whose friends had died.

A HIGHWAY ROBBER IS BETTER THAN A MEDIUM. AT LEAST THEY ROB THEIR VICTIMS OUT IN THE OPEN

DID YOU KNOW...

Spiritualists are still popular in the 2020s. A woman in England had a horse that looked unhappy. A spiritualist was called in. She said she called on the horse's mother to talk to the unhappy animal. Saddle-y we don't know if it worked. The horse said, 'Nay.'

OOOOH EEEE OOOOH EEE

SERIOUSLY?

MORE MACBETH MYSTERY

You would think that by today the idea of ghosts would be just a joke, not real. We have so many cameras and bright lights. A ghost-faker will find it difficult to tell a trick tale. Yet they go on. That old Macbeth Curse lives on in places like Oldham, Lancashire. In the Oldham Coliseum Theatre there is said to be the ghost of a dead actor, Harold Norman.

Harold played Macbeth there in January 1947. He mocked the Macbeth curse. Norman was accidentally stabbed with a real sword.

The wound became infected, and he died of blood poisoning on 27 February in Oldham Royal Infirmary.

Harold's ghost can still be seen sitting in the theatre seats – watching plays. He usually appears on a Thursday – the day he died. Or doors bang shut in an empty corridor, things fall off shelves in an empty room. Dogs are too afraid to enter an office under the stage.

But he also seems to appear when tickets are selling badly. People WANT to see a ghost and they buy tickets to see Harold Norman, not just the play.

EPILOGUE

Many towns have their own ghost stories and people pay to wander round in the dark to hear about hauntings. They are just stories. Some are just silly. But others are just horrible. One of the most horrible is set in the City of York.

It is the story of a teacher called Mr George Pimm.

In the early days of Queen Victoria, you had to pay to go to school. Poor parents couldn't afford it. They went off to work and took the children with them. Then the laws changed and said children could NOT go into factories and mines.

Victoria's ministers came up with a new plan to get those poor kids off the streets.

So, the Ragged Schools were set up. They didn't have SATs but they were still as horrible as today's schools. Charles Dickens visited one and said...

*T*hose who are too ragged, wretched, filthy and forlorn to enter any other place were invited to come in here and find some people willing to teach them something.

I visited one Ragged School with two or three miserable rooms, upstairs in a miserable house. In the best of these, the pupils in the girls' school were being taught to read and write. The appearance of this room was sad but there was some hope. The room next door was a worse place.

The narrow, low space at the back was so foul and stifling as to be almost unbearable. Huddled together on a bench about the room were a crowd of boys.

They were aged from mere infants to young men; sellers of fruit, herbs, matches, flints; sleepers under the dry arches of bridges; young thieves and beggars.

And in York the child-catcher in chief was Mr Pimm. He was paid to take children off the streets of the city. His school was in the Bedern area.

THE MORE KIDS, THE MORE MONEY

He had to feed them and keep them in clothes. But if he gave them little food and cheap, chilly clothing he would make more money for himself. That's what he did.

Winter came and the shivering students started to die of cold and hunger. The ground was too hard to dig their graves, so Mr Pimm started to store them away in a cupboard. If he told anyone they were dead then he'd lose the money he was paid for each child.

THAT WAS WHEN I HEARD THEM CALLING TO ME. LAUGHING. TORMENTING. SCREAMING. I'M NOT MAD. I'M NOT. THEY REALLY WERE COMING BACK FROM THE DEAD

The teacher took a knife to attack the children, and that is when the doctors came to take him away to lock him up.

Today, if you go to Bedern in York you might hear the soft laughter of children. And as you walk down the cobbled road you may feel the small, cold hand of a child take hold of yours.

They are the ghosts of Bedern Ragged School. The victims of Mr Pimm.

He is as true as Anne Boleyn with her head tucked underneath her arm, screaming skulls, talking to Auntie Gladys through a medium or the phantom *Flying Dutchman* ship.

There WAS a York Ragged School, which opened in 1850, but that was on Marygate and that is nowhere near Bedern. If there WERE ghostly children, wouldn't they be on Marygate?

And George Pimm was said to have died in 1858. But there is no record of his death or burial.

Fakes, mistakes and simply stories. That's ghosts for you. In all of history none have been true.

Sleep well.

INTERESTING INDEX

Where will you find dreadful disasters, ghosts and hunting heads in an index? In a *Horrible Histories* book, of course!

TERRY DEARY

Terry Deary was born at a very early age, so long ago he can't remember. But his mother, who was there at the time, says he was born in Sunderland, north-east England, in 1946 – so it's not true that he writes all *Horrible Histories* from memory. At school he was a horrible child only interested in playing football and giving teachers a hard time. His history lessons were so boring and so badly taught, that he learned to loathe the subject. *Horrible Histories* is his revenge.

MARTIN BROWN

Martin Brown was born in Melbourne, on the proper side of the world. Ever since he can remember he's been drawing. His dad used to bring back huge sheets of paper from work and Martin would fill them with doodles and little figures. Then, quite suddenly, with food and water, he grew up, moved to the UK and found work doing what he's always wanted to do: drawing doodles and little figures.

COLLECT THEM ALL!

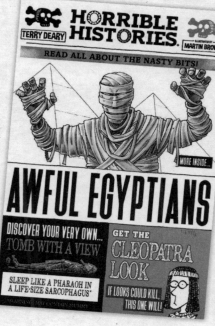

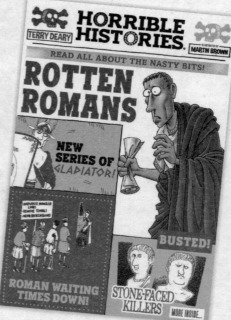

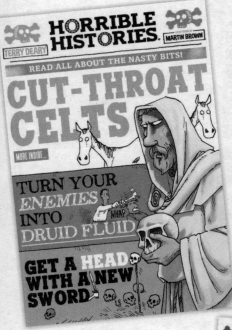